W9-BLI-895

megabat

Daniel Misumi has just moved to a new house. It's big and old and far away from his friends and his life before. And it's haunted . . . or is it?

Megabat was just napping on a papaya one day when he was stuffed in a box and shipped halfway across the world. Now he's living in an old house far from home, feeling sorry for himself and accidentally scaring the people who live there.

Daniel realizes it's not a ghost in his new house. It's a bat. He can talk. And he's actually kind of cute.

Megabat realizes that not every human wants to whack him with a broom. This one shares his smooshfruit.

Add some buttermelon, juice boxes, a lightsaber and a common enemy, and you've got a friendship in the making!

Tundra Books, an imprint of Penguin Random House Canada Young Readers,
a Penguin Random House Company

Library and Archives Canada Cataloguing in Publication
Humphrey, Anna, 1979–, author
Megabat / Anna Humphrey ; [illustrations by] Kass Reich.
Issued in print and electronic formats.
ISBN 978-0-7352-6257-7 (hardcover).—ISBN 978-0-7352-6258-4 (EPUB)
I. Reich, Kass, illustrator II. Title.

PS8615.U457M44 2018   jC813'.6   C2017-904328-5
                                               C2017-904329-3

Published simultaneously in the United States of America by Tundra Books
of Northern New York, an imprint of Penguin Random House Canada Young Readers,
a Penguin Random House Company

Library of Congress Control Number: 2017945613

Edited by Samantha Swenson
Designed by Andrew Roberts
The artwork in this book was rendered in graphite.
The text was set in Caslon 540 LT Std.

Printed and bound in the United States of America

www.penguinrandomhouse.ca

1   2   3   4   5   22   21   20   19   18

Penguin
Random House
tundra   TUNDRA BOOKS

ANNA HUMPHREY

illustrated by KASS REICH

MEGA BAT

tundra

For my neighbors.
You made Kitchener home.

NO BUTTERMELONS

Daniel Misumi hated his new house. He hated the vines that crept up the red brick and the way the peaks over the upstairs windows looked like angry eyebrows. He hated the creaky floors and the weird wallpaper... but most of all, he hated his new attic bedroom—especially when he discovered a ghostly creature was living there.

Daniel's first clue about the creature was the mysterious puddle at the top of the stairs.

"Oof!" he said, landing on his bum. It was moving day, and he'd been carrying a box of Lego. Pieces crashed to the floor and skittered under the furniture like beetles afraid of the light.

Daniel stood up and examined his wet shorts. "Mom!" he called. "There's a puddle on my floor!"

Daniel found his mom in the bathroom. She was busy unpacking her bottles of relaxing bubble bath. "Just what we need." She sighed. "A leak in the roof on our first day."

Daniel's father was summoned. He

made grim faces at the ceiling and said things like "Welllllll…" and "Let's see…" but no hole or crack was discovered.

"Maybe it's not water," Daniel said as they mopped up the puddle. "It could be corrosive liquid leaking from a rusty pipe." In such an old house, he wouldn't have been surprised.

Daniel eyed the ceiling suspiciously, but his dad just said they'd deal with it later.

So Daniel tried to put the puddle out of his mind, but later that night, when he was drifting off to sleep…

"Gots buttermelons? Hmmm?"

His eyes shot open.

"Buttermelons? Nope? None?"

The voice was small and quivering, and if he hadn't been so terrified, Daniel might have noticed how filled with sadness it was.

He pulled the blankets over his head. At first it seemed to work. The room stayed silent for a long time. So long that Daniel almost convinced himself he'd imagined the whole thing.

"Buttermelons? Peeze! None? Noooooooooo."

The voice came again, even more quivery than before. Plus, now there was a strange flapping sound.

Daniel sat up, turned on the bedside light and raised his arms in a fierce karate move. He looked around the room.

There was nothing—just his furniture
and unpacked boxes.

He kicked his covers off and backed
toward the stairs. But—"Oof!" he slipped
in the mystery puddle again. "Uh. Ah!"
He tumbled backward down the stairs.

"Daniel!" his mother appeared in her pajamas. Her hair was sticking up in a million directions. "Are you okay?"

"There's a ghost… in my room." He scrambled toward the safety of his parents' bed.

His dad sighed.

"I promise there's no ghost," his mother said. To prove it, she marched up the stairs. Daniel was expecting her to yell down, "See? Nothing here," but instead—*THUNK*.

His dad ran up behind her.

"Daniel?" he called back. "Your mother slipped! Why's the floor all wet?"

"I *told* you." Daniel said. He climbed under his parents' covers. "That puddle keeps appearing. I think this house is haunted. We need to leave."

"Oh, for Pete's sake," his dad said, coming back down. "We'll call a roofer in the morning. For now, back to your own bed, mister. It's one hundred percent ghost-free up there."

So Daniel climbed the stairs. He lay awake with his ears and eyes wide open, but he didn't hear the voice again—at least, not that night.

2

THE BAT

The next morning, Daniel got up at the first sign of light. He stepped around the puddle and ran down the stairs to safety.

His mother found him asleep on the couch an hour later. "Rise and shine." She ruffled his hair. "We've got a lot of unpacking to do before school starts."

Daniel grumbled. The last thing he

wanted to be reminded of was school. Back in Toronto, he'd had two best friends and a spot on the soccer team— but at his new school, he wouldn't even know where the bathrooms were—let alone who to play with at recess. It was going to be horrible.

Daniel closed his eyes again, but moments later, something brushed his neck. The ghost! He leapt up, only to find his father holding a feather duster.

"Ticklish much?" he teased. "Can you clean the shelves in the dining room?" Daniel groaned, but he did what he was told.

As long as he didn't have to go back to the attic, he'd do anything.

Daniel sorted spoons, he organized underwear, he unboxed baking pans... but it was no use.

"Honey," his mom said, after lunch. "Why don't you take your dessert up to your room and play?"

"That's okay!" he said quickly. "I'll alphabetize the spice rack!" But his mom insisted.

She put a plate in his hand. It had a delicious-looking piece of jelly roll on it. Daniel doubted he'd be able to enjoy it in his room, but he knew that if he mentioned the ghost again, his parents would say he was being silly. So he took the plate and went upstairs.

When he reached the main floor landing, Daniel edged the attic door open and paused. There was a very faint sound. *Drip. Drip. Drip.*

He tiptoed up a few steps.

"Doooooooooh. Mine is all aloooooone."

It was the voice again.

"Mine is got no bests and noooo friends." The words were followed by

the dripping noise, faster now.
Dripdripdripdrip.

Daniel reminded himself to breathe.
If there was something lurking in his
bedroom, he was going to have to face it
eventually. He forced his feet to keep
climbing.

"Hello?" he called. "I know you're
there! So show yourself." Daniel froze,
listening—but everything was still.
Even the dripping sound had stopped.
"I won't harm you," he added.

Daniel walked around the puddle and
into the middle of the room.

Sniff. Sniff.

The softest little breathing sounds
were coming from somewhere in the

ceiling beams. Daniel squinted into the dark space and saw it. At first, he thought it was a large mouse… only its eyes were much too big. Also, it was hanging upside down. Then the creature shifted, and he saw the ripple and sheen of its wings.

A bat!

THE LAND OF
PAPAYA PREMIUM

Daniel had touched a garter snake once, and his best friend in Toronto had a gerbil named Gopher that he liked... but bats were different.

"Please don't suck my blood," he said, even though he didn't *really* expect the bat to understand.

"Yours said what?" the voice answered.

"I said, please don't suck my blood," Daniel repeated, in the direction of the bat, just in case it *was* the bat talking.

"Blood? Yours is drinking blood? Dust-gusting!" spat the voice.

"No," Daniel said. "*I* don't drink blood. *You* do. If you're a bat. Are you?"

"Undoubtedly." The creature edged into the light. "A bat. But not a dust-gusting blood-sucking bat."

Daniel was no bat expert, but something about the shape of the face made him guess it was a boy bat.

The bat sniffed again. He had a tiny pink heart-shaped nose, almost like a rabbit's. Suddenly, his eyes went even wider than before.

"Yours gots red smoosh-fruit!" the bat exclaimed. He swooped. Daniel threw his arms over his head to protect himself and the plastic plate and jelly roll he'd been holding went flying.

The bat landed near the dessert. He

sniffed again, then plunged his snout into the jelly, snorffling like a pig at a trough.

While the bat ate, Daniel got a closer look. He was tiny—smaller than a blue jay and only a little bigger than a butterfly. He had a furry body and large, leathery wings.

When the bat finished, he looked up and burped loudly.

"Scu-zzi," he said politely, then he flapped back into the rafters and hung upside town, tilting his head.

There was a long, awkward silence while Daniel tried to figure out what a person was supposed to say to a talking bat. Finally, he decided on the obvious.

"I'm Daniel," he said. "What's your name?"

"Yours is a Daniel?" the bat said, tilting his head to the other side.

"Yes," he confirmed. "And you?"

"A bat," he answered.

"Yeah, but what's your *name*?" Daniel pressed.

"A bat," the bat repeated.

"Okay." Daniel shrugged. "I'll call you Bat then."

There was another long silence. Finally, the bat gave a small, annoyed sigh. "A Daniel gots more smoosh-fruit?" He tapped his tiny talon.

Daniel knew there was still half a jelly roll, but his mom wouldn't give him more before dinner—especially not if he told her it was for a talking bat.

"I can get more later," Daniel said.

Bat hunched up his wings, clearly disappointed.

"I could probably get you some

watermelon now, though." Daniel's parents loved when he ate fruit.

Bat's large ears perked up. "Buttermelon?" he said.

"*Water*melon," Daniel corrected.

"*Butter*melon," Bat insisted.

"Okay, buttermelon," Daniel said. It hardly mattered what they called it. "But first, are you the one who keeps making the puddle?"

"Undoubtedly," Bat replied forlornly. "A bat is dripping. From a great sadness."

"You mean crying?" Daniel asked.

"Dripping," the bat repeated, "from mine eyes."

"Why are you sad?" Daniel sat down

on his bed. He wasn't afraid anymore, only curious.

"A bat is many miles from mine home," the bat replied.

"Are you lost?" Daniel asked.

"Lost," said the bat. "And all alone." Then he started to cry again. *Drip, drip, drip.*

"I'm a long way from home too," Daniel said. "Well, three hours by car. But my family's here, so I guess I'm not all alone like you."

This only made the bat cry harder.

"Where did you live before?" Daniel asked.

"Mine home is the land of Papaya Premium," the bat said.

"Where's that?" Daniel asked. He'd gotten an A in geography, but he'd never heard of it.

The bat got a faraway look in his eye. "The land of Papaya Premium is where the shore meets the sea so blue. Where the parrots squawkety squawk and the piggy elephants romp in the raining forest. It's being where the waterfalls burble and the whiffy orchid flowers spread sweetish stink."

Daniel held up a hand to stop him because, otherwise, it seemed like the bat might go on all day.

"I mean, where is it?" he said. "Like, on a map."

Bat frowned.

"Or a globe?" Daniel tried. That didn't help.

"A blobe?" the bat said. He seemed to like that word. "Blobe, blobe, blobbedy-blobe."

"Never mind," Daniel said. He shouldn't have expected a bat to know second grade geography.

Still, one thing was certain: wherever Papaya Premium was, Bat had to go back. If Daniel's mom knew a bat was living in the attic—well, it wouldn't be living there long. She'd get his dad to chase it out or—worse—call an exterminator.

If Bat couldn't tell Daniel where Papaya Premium was, he'd need to figure it out himself. And, in the meantime, keep Bat from crying before he flooded the whole house.

"Wait here," Daniel said. "I'll get your buttermelon."

4

THE LIBRARY

Even though Bat flew in circles and
smacked his leathery lips when he saw
the watermelon, it wasn't long before he
was right back to dripping—or crying—
whatever you wanted to call it. Daniel
was pretty sure neither of them slept a
wink that night.

Daniel needed to get Bat home, and
soon. He asked his parents about the

land of Papaya Premium at breakfast, but they'd never heard of it either.

"Who told you about that?" his mother asked.

"Just a friend," he answered.

"Oh," she replied, hopefully. "Did you meet one of the kids next door?"

Daniel had seen the neighbor kids twice… once while carrying in boxes and again when he took out the trash. There was a girl about his age and a boy a little younger. He'd thought about waving, but they looked busy.

"No. Jason told me about Papaya Premium before we left Toronto," he lied. His mom looked discouraged.

Daniel felt discouraged too. He couldn't even look up Papaya Premium online because the Internet wasn't set up. Then he remembered: there was another way.

"Can you take me to the library?" he asked.

"Sure," his mom said. "The roofers

are coming to look at that leak in your room anyway. Why don't we go now?"

Daniel had almost forgotten about the "leak." He couldn't tell his parents what was really causing it. But he also couldn't leave Bat to be discovered by the roofers.

"Wait! I just need to get my—um—bookmark," Daniel said. He ran up to the attic.

"Bat!" he called.

Bat, who'd been fast asleep after a long night of keeping Daniel awake, blinked his giant eyes open.

"I'm going to the library to get information about your land. You need to come with me. Workers are on their way. If they find you here, they might hurt you."

"Does theys gots brooms?" Bat asked, trembling.

"Ummm, I don't think so," Daniel answered. "But they probably have hammers and saws and things."

Bat flew toward Daniel and latched on to one of his fingers with his feet, hanging upside down. Each foot had five tiny claws. They were sharp and grippy, but smoother than Daniel would have expected.

"Hide in my shirt pocket and stay quiet," Daniel said. Then he remembered what he'd told his mom. He grabbed his Star Wars bookmark. "Hold this," he said, tucking it into his pocket with Bat.

When they got to the library, Daniel's mom went to sign up for library cards. Meanwhile, Daniel found a computer.

It was in a corner facing the wall, so it was safe to let Bat out.

"If anyone comes, hide behind the bookmark," Daniel told Bat.

Daniel started with an internet search for "Papaya Premium," but all he got were recipes for smoothies.

Then he had an idea. Bat didn't always call things by the right names…

"You said there are *waterfalls*, right? And *orchids*? *Parrots*? A *raining forest* and *piggy elephants*? And it's near the *sea*…" Daniel entered those key words instead. The computer auto-corrected a few.

"Oh! You probably meant *pygmy* elephants!" he said. "And the *rainforest*. Borneo!" he announced, looking at the

top search results. "Is your homeland
Borneo?"

Bat was busy staring at the picture on
Daniel's bookmark.

"I think it's probably Borneo," Daniel concluded. "But that's on the other side of the world!"

"Is a bat?" Bat asked, tilting the bookmark so Daniel could see.

"No," he laughed. "That's Darth Vader." But he could understand how the bat might make that mistake. Darth Vader wore all black and his mask had a snouty look. "You know... from Star Wars. May the Force be with you!"

But, of course, Bat didn't know a thing about Star Wars.

"I'll show you later. Right now, look." He pointed to some images of Borneo on the screen. "Is that home?"

"Undoubtedly." Bat nodded. "There is being the raining forest… and the waterfalls are very much a-same."

"Good," Daniel said. "It's Borneo. Now we just need to get you back. How did you get here, anyway? Did you fly all that way?"

Bat shook his head. "A Bat traveled in a crate marked with the name of mine land: Papaya Premium."

"But why?" Daniel asked.

"Mine was napping on a tree one sunny day when, out of nowheres, mine sleeping-papaya was plucked and made to plummet into a crate filled with mores papayas," said the bat, "which mine gobbled most hungrily. A bat journeyed many days. First in a rolling rectangle, then in the belly of a roaring beast. One day, mine arrived in a noisy land, filled with fruits mine could smell but not reach." Bat winced as he remembered this torture.

"At last," he went on, "a Daniel with

white hair carried mine crate away. Before longish, the Daniel opened the crate, screamed shriekily and tried to flatten a Bat with a broom." Bat trembled. "But mine made a daring upward exscape. And sincely, mine has been all alone—until yours arrived."

Daniel took a minute to put the pieces of Bat's story together. Suddenly, he remembered a jar of chunky papaya jam that had been left by the old owner as a welcome gift. She must have been the white-haired "Daniel" who had opened the crate, screamed and chased Bat with a broom.

"You know," Daniel told the bat, "Not all humans are called Daniels. I think that one's name was Mrs. Jenkins or something."

"Mrs-Jenkins-or-Something is a great villain," said Bat somberly. "Her thwacky broom is most terrible."

Daniel was going to point out that Mrs. Jenkins was probably just a sweet old lady—but he noticed his mother coming. Quickly, he tucked Bat into his pocket.

MEGABAT

That night, while his parents kept
unpacking, Daniel settled in on the
couch in the family room. Bat, who
was sitting atop a cushion, slurped apple
juice through a bendy straw and
watched with wide eyes as Luke
Skywalker learned to wield a lightsaber.
Meanwhile, Daniel read.

He'd brought home three big books

about bats from the library. Already, he'd learned that Bat was a fruit bat. Fruit bats live in warm climates. They have a strong sense of smell and a long tongue that they roll out when eating fruit nectar, then roll back in—like the tape measure Daniel's mom used for woodworking.

"It says here that fruit bats live in colonies with sub-groups of eight or nine bats, like families," Daniel said. That explained why Bat had been so lonely in the attic.

"Undoubtedly," Bat said, not taking his eyes off the TV.

"And sometimes fruit bats are called flying foxes or megabats. *Megabat*." Daniel smiled. It was a powerful name for such a tiny creature. "It's almost like a superhero name," he said.

"A superhero name," Bat repeated.

"Like, a good guy name," Daniel explained. "Luke Skywalker is kind of like a superhero. Because he fights the bad guy, Darth Vader."

At that, Bat's ears perked up. "A Megabat is like Luke Skywalker?" he asked.

"I don't know," Daniel laughed. "Do you have a lightsaber?"

Bat glanced down. His tongue flicked in and out of his mouth in excitement. Using the claws on his wingtips, he pulled the bendy straw out of his drink box and poked Daniel's arm with it.

"Not bad." Daniel grinned. "I bet with a little training, Megabat could totally defeat Darth Vader."

By then the movie credits were rolling. Daniel knew his parents would be coming to tell him it was bedtime soon.

"But for now we should probably get some sleep. I think I figured out a way to get you home… but we'll have to wait until tomorrow. Here, I'll throw that out." Daniel reached for the drink box straw— but Bat wouldn't let go.

"Unhand mine lightsaber!" the bat shrieked so loudly that Daniel was worried his parents would hear.

"Okay, okay…" Daniel shook his head. "Keep it. Come on, Bat. Let's go upstairs." He held out his hand as a perch.

"Who is this Bat yours speaks of?" Bat ruffled his wings with an air of great importance. "Mine is *Mega*bat."

"Sorry… I meant, come on, *Megabat*." Daniel tried to hide his smile.

Megabat flew to Daniel's finger and hung upside down, still clutching the straw in his wingtips. The friends went upstairs and slept soundly for the first time in days.

THE CASSEROLE DISH
OF DOOM

Daniel and Megabat got up early to work on the plan. It was simple, really. Megabat had traveled from Borneo in a crate of papayas… so to return him, all they needed to do was put to him in another box and mail him back.

"Of course," Daniel told Megabat, "it can't be just any box. It needs to be strong and comfortable. It's a long trip."

Thankfully, there were plenty of boxes in Daniel's house. After breakfast, Daniel slipped Megabat into his pocket and they went in search of the perfect one. They finally found it in the basement. It was an old apple cider box that had dividers inside. They'd make perfect walls for creating different rooms.

Daniel was carrying the perfect box upstairs, with Megabat still tucked in his pocket, when his mother stopped him in the kitchen.

"Sweetie, do me a favor? Run this over to Patricia next door." Daniel's mom was drying a casserole dish with a tea towel. "It's from the lasagna she brought over."

Daniel sighed. He knew what his mom was trying to do. The lasagna-dish house was where the two kids lived: the girl and the boy he'd seen before. Daniel's mother was hoping he'd meet them. She was dreaming they'd become friends—*best* friends. Well, it wasn't going to happen. Daniel's friends were in Toronto.

He didn't want to make new ones.

But Daniel's mom held the dish out insistently.

"This'll only take a second," he whispered to Megabat as they headed out the door. He'd already decided to leave the dish on the porch.

Unfortunately, the lady next door was out watering her garden. What's more, she had the same idea as his mom.

"Oh, hello," she said, from under her floppy sun hat. "You must be Daniel. I'm Patricia."

"Nice to meet you," he said, then he held the dish out toward her.

"Just put it on the steps," Patricia said with a smile. "You know, my kids are in the backyard. Their names are Talia and Jamie. They've been dying to meet you."

"Oh. I'm kind of—" He was going to say "busy" but she didn't let him.

"Just pop around back for a second," she suggested.

Daniel knew it would be rude to say no. He'd just say hi, he told himself. Then he'd go work on Megabat's box.

"Hello?" Daniel called as he made his way past the garbage bins at the side of the house. Nobody answered and soon he saw why. The girl was jumping on a trampoline. The springs were making a rhythmic twanging noise. Her reddish pigtails were flapping like wings. She got higher and higher, then suddenly she

flipped, landed and got ready to do it again.

Meanwhile, the boy was nailing pieces of wood together. Between the hammering and the twanging, the kids couldn't hear him.

Daniel was just about to turn and leave, when—"Oh!" The girl dropped to her bum. "Hi," she said. "You're the new neighbor. Jamie!" she shouted to her brother. "Say hi to the new neighbor."

The boy looked up but didn't stop hammering.

"I'm Talia," the girl said, climbing down from the trampoline. "That's Jamie. You can ignore him if you want. He's busy being cruel to animals."

That got the boy's attention. "I'm not being cruel," Jamie said. "I'm defending our yard from pigeon poop by building a trap." He motioned to the roof, where at least two dozen pigeons were perched. They glanced down nervously every few seconds, bobbing their heads. "They're always doing their business on my bike."

"So put your bike in the shed," Talia answered, exasperated. "Anyway, what's your name?" she asked Daniel.

Daniel told her, then he started mumbling about how he had to get home. He hadn't made it very far, though, when the screen door opened and Patricia stepped out carrying home-made popsicles. "Who wants a fruit pop?" she called. "They're banana, blueberry, passion fruit."

Jamie made a gross-out face. Megabat, on the other hand, started to squirm with excitement.

"Did hers say *passion fruit*?" came the bat's voice from Daniel's shirt pocket. He crossed his arm over his chest to muffle the words. Thankfully, Patricia was too busy telling Jamie to "watch his manners" to hear the odd little voice—but Talia gave Daniel a strange look.

He cleared his throat loudly. "Sorry," he said. "I just really love passion fruit."

"Well, that's nice to hear," said Patricia. She handed a fruit pop to Daniel.

"Anyway," Daniel said, after she'd

gone inside. "I really should go now because—"

"What was that?" Talia pointed to his chest.

"What?" Daniel asked.

"*That!*"

Daniel glanced down at his pocket just in time to see the bat's long pink tongue dart out, lick his fruit pop, then dart back in.

"Ummmm…" Daniel stalled.

"There's something alive in there." Talia came closer. "It's squirming." By now, even Jamie was interested.

"It's just my pet," Daniel said.

"I love animals!" Talia exclaimed. "Is it a mouse?"

Megabat licked the ice pop again. This time his pointy ears stuck out too.

"It's a… fruit bat," Daniel said, deciding to leave out the talking part. "But don't tell, okay? It's a secret fruit bat. I'm letting it go soon."

"Is it injured?" Talia asked. Her voice was filled with concern. "One time I found a pigeon with a hurt wing, and I nursed it back to health."

"Which was great." Jamie rolled his eyes. "Because now it extra loves us, so it extra poops in our yard."

"Anyway," Daniel went on. "My bat needs help. I should go."

"Okay," Talia said. "But if I can help too, tell me. I'm good with animals."

Jamie picked up his hammer again. "Just wear gloves," he said. "It's probably crawling with parasites."

"Like you'd know." Talia put her hands on her hips.

Daniel didn't feel like sticking around for their fight. "Good to meet you," he said. Then he pushed Megabat's head back into his pocket and ran home.

THE BOX

Back in the attic, Daniel got straight to work on the box.

"This'll be your sleeping area," he explained, showing Megabat one section.

"And, over here, I'm putting three oranges, two bananas and some cut-up watermelon. And I got you these." He held up some juice boxes. "In case you get thirsty."

The bat licked the outside of a juice box then tried to bite through it with his front fangs.

"You use a straw, remember?" Daniel pointed to the little straw wrapped in plastic, but Megabat scoffed. He went to retrieve his own straw, then he clutched it in his wingtips and charged at the juice box, smacking into it, bending the straw, and knocking himself backward.

Daniel laughed. "You need to stick it in this little hole." He showed Megabat the foil-covered part at the top. The bat nodded then charged again. It took many tries but, eventually, the straw went in and they both cheered like they'd just defeated the Death Star.

"Honey?" Daniel's mom called. "What are you doing up there?"

"Umm… just reading," he said.

"It must be a funny book. I could hear you laughing all the way downstairs."

"Sorry," he said.

"Don't be," his mom answered. "Dinner in two minutes, all right?"

Daniel waited until he heard the sound of his mom's feet going back down the stairs. "I'll bring you part of my jelly roll after dinner. Then we can finish making your box, okay?"

"Oka-hay," the bat said, trying out the new word. Megabat backed up, then

added a double spin twist before
spearing the juice box again. Daniel
grinned and shook his head. He was
going to miss that crazy little fruit bat
when he sent him home.

Dinner was oniony meatloaf, but Daniel wolfed it down. He didn't want to miss a minute of his last night with Megabat. He was busy loading the dishwasher as fast as possible when the doorbell rang.

"Daniel!" his mom sang out. "It's Talia from next door. She wants to play. Isn't that nice?"

Daniel wasn't sure it was "nice." She was probably only interested in his secret fruit bat.

"Ummm…" Daniel slid another plate into the dishwasher as Talia followed his mom into the kitchen. "Maybe tomorrow. I'm kind of busy tonight."

"Daniel!" his mom gasped. "Talia came all the way over to play." She said it like "all the way over" was across the Sahara Desert and not just a few steps from next door.

Daniel shot his mom a pleading look, which she answered with her "do not be rude" stare.

Daniel closed the dishwasher, handed Talia a slice of jelly roll and showed her toward the stairs. He just had to hope that, by some miracle, Megabat would know enough to keep quiet so she wouldn't find out he could talk.

"Wooohoo! Yours is broughtten smoosh-fruit!"

Megabat *did not* know enough to keep quiet. Not even a little bit. "Oooooooh. Double smoosh fruits." He eyed the plate Talia was carrying. "And ladyfriend."

"Who's up here?" Talia asked. She dropped her backpack to the floor, then her mouth dropped open as she looked around and saw no one.

"Don't scream, okay?" Daniel warned. He pointed to the ceiling.

"Like I'd scream." Talia put her hands on her hips. "But I still don't see anyone."

"Look closer. Megabat, this is Talia. Talia, that's Megabat."

At the sound of his name, Megabat did an awkward upside-down bow, unfurling his wing in front of him. "It is being an honor to meeting yours," he said formally.

Talia took a small, startled step back but didn't even come close to screaming. "That's a talking bat," she said.

"Yup." Daniel flopped down on his bed. "Trust me, he never *stops* talking."

"Are you hurt, little bat?" Talia held out her hand. "I brought some

bandages." Megabat flew into her palm and started to rub his ears against her cheek like a purring cat. He obviously liked girls.

"He's not hurt," Daniel said. "He's lost." He told Talia the whole story, ending with the part about how he was going to mail Megabat home.

"That's a good idea," Talia said. "I mean, before anyone else finds out he's here. I made Jamie swear not to tell, but if he learns your bat can talk, he won't be able to keep his mouth shut."

"It seems like you've thought of everything," she said, examining the different sections of the box. Daniel felt his cheeks glow with pride. "Except…"

She flipped the top flap closed. "Where are you going to mail it to?"

"I already told you," Daniel answered. "Borneo."

"Yeah, but *where* in Borneo? It's a big place." She paused. "Also, who's going to open the box when he gets there?"

Daniel hadn't even thought of that!

"I don't know anyone in Borneo," Daniel said. "Do you?"

"No," Talia said. "But that's okay."

Minutes later, using Daniel's dad's phone they'd found and copied the address of a papaya farm in East Kalimantan, Borneo, and had decided to address the package to "Farmer Bambang" whose name they'd found on a blog. Finally, they wrote FRAGILE and OPEN IMMEDIATELY in big letters.

The box was completely ready.

"What do you want to do now?" Daniel asked. There was more than an hour before bedtime.

"I don't know," Talia said. "It's your last night here, Megabat. What do *you* want to do?"

"Megabat will be watching *Star Wars*," the bat said without hesitation. "And drinking juice of the apple."

It was exactly what they'd done the night before, but Daniel didn't mind.

Daniel made popcorn and got Megabat three juice boxes. Talia and the bat both gasped when the Millennium Falcon went into hyperspace and covered their eyes at the parts with Darth Vader… and even though, at first, Daniel had wished that the girl from next door hadn't come over, in the end he was glad.

THE POST OFFICE

The next morning, Talia came to help
Daniel carry the box to the post office.

She brought a red wagon to put it in and some magazines for Megabat to look at on his trip. When everything was in the box, she held out her hand for Megabat. He flew into it and she let him nuzzle against her cheek.

Meanwhile, Daniel stood by awkwardly. He hated goodbyes. Unfortunately, Megabat didn't give him much choice. He landed on Daniel's head, leaned over and licked him right across the face with his super long tongue.

"Ewww!" Daniel laughed and wiped off the bat spit. "Is that how they say goodbye in Papaya Premium?"

Megabat flew to the edge of his box,

gave them both a salute with one wingtip and hopped in.

Daniel had a fluttery feeling in his tummy all the way to the post office and while they waited in line. When it was their turn, Talia carefully lifted the box onto the counter.

"All the way to Borneo, eh?" the postal worker said, as she measured the box. "Regular or airmail express?" Daniel chose express.

"And what are the contents?" The woman pulled out a form with tiny lettering on it.

Obviously they couldn't tell her the box contained a talking fruit bat!

"Just some fruit…" Daniel said,

thinking fast. "And a few other things," he added, for the sake of honesty.

"Sorry." The postal worker pushed the box back toward them. "You can't mail fruit internationally. All kinds of pests can travel that way."

"But—" Daniel started to argue.

The postal worker glanced at the long lineup behind them.

Talia calmly picked up their package. "Come on," she said.

Back in Daniel's room, Talia pulled off the packing tape. They could hear the flapping of Megabat's wings grow louder. The second the box opened, he burst forth, singing out, "Megabat is returned! Bat brothers and sisters! Megabat is back in Papaya—" He stopped and looked around. "Megabat is not returned to Papaya Premium?" he asked. He came to roost on the edge of the box, tucked his wings around himself and peered up, looking very small indeed.

Daniel crouched down. "Sorry, Megabat. We can't mail you home." A large tear gathered in one corner of Megabat's eye, slid down his furry face and hit the floor with a splash. Daniel felt like he might cry too.

"It's okay, Megabat," Talia said softly. "We'll find another way. Actually, it's a lucky thing, because I just realized:

We've only had time to watch the *first* Star Wars movie. Did you know there are more?"

Another tear was just starting to roll out of Megabat's eye, but at Talia's words, he blinked hopefully. "Mores Star Wars?"

"Well, yeah." Daniel followed Talia's lead. "We watched *A New Hope*, twice... but you haven't even met the Ewoks yet."

So they spent the afternoon watching Hans Solo, Luke Skywalker and Princess Leia fight the evil galactic empire—but the whole time, they were wondering—was there *really* another way to get Megabat home?

THE ESCAPE

By that night, Daniel and Talia were no
closer to coming up with a plan, and
things were looking more desperate—
not to mention drippy. Star Wars
Episodes V and VI kept Megabat busy
all afternoon, but as soon as it got dark
he hung upside down from the rafter and
rocked back and forth, crying big,
splashy tears.

Daniel dumped out a bin of stuffed
animals and placed the empty container
under Megabat, then he crawled into
bed, feeling almost as sad.

Drip. Drip. Drip. Drip. Drip. Drip.

It took Daniel hours to get to sleep, and just after he finally had—"Daniel?"

Both his parents were standing at the top of the stairs, squinting into the darkness.

"Mmhmm?" he said blearily.

"I'm turning on the light, okay?" said Daniel's dad.

Daniel blinked, then he gasped. His parents were standing directly underneath Megabat's perch, staring up into the rafters.

"Has the roof been leaking for a while?" his mom asked, looking down at the stuffed animal bucket, which Daniel saw was overflowing with bat tears.

Daniel nodded.

"It's good you put a bucket there, but, Daniel, you should have come down to tell us. It's coming right through the floor," his mom said.

From where Daniel was sitting in bed, he could just make out the sheen of Megabat's eyes. When his parents weren't looking, he raised one finger to his lips. "Shhhhhh," he said.

"Yours said what?" came a voice.

"What was that?" Daniel's mom asked.

"Um. Oh." Daniel reached into the big pile of stuffed animals on the floor and pulled out a walrus. "That was Wally the Talking Walrus. It's got batteries."

"It does?" his mother asked. She gave

her head a little shake. "Anyway. I'll get the mop," she said, then she turned to his dad. "Could you empty this bucket?"

"Megabat!" Daniel whispered furiously, as soon as his parents had left. "Come here this second."

"Shouty, shouty," Megabat complained, but he came to roost on Daniel's outstretched finger all the same.

"You need to hide," Daniel said. "My parents will be back any minute." Then he did the only thing he could think of that was guaranteed to keep Megabat silent and out of sight. He opened one of his windows and placed him on the outer ledge. "Wait there," he said, sliding the window shut.

Between mopping the puddle, cleaning up what had spilled down the stairs and replacing the container with a bigger bucket, half an hour passed before Daniel's family was ready to go back to bed.

As soon as his parents left, Daniel ran to the window and opened it. "They're gone," he whispered. "You can come back in."

But there was no answer—because there was no Megabat, just the big, dark night sky with the thinnest sliver of moon.

For more than an hour, Daniel sat by the window whispering Megabat's name into the darkness, but the bat didn't return. First thing the next morning, he asked his mom if he could go to Talia's house. "Of course," she answered, grinning into her toast.

"Megabat's lost," Daniel blurted the second Talia opened the door.

He told her how the bat had run away.

"He's a wild animal," Talia said. "It's normal that he'd want to explore."

"I guess," Daniel agreed. "But we need to find him. He doesn't know this country. He could get lost or hurt."

They started their search for Megabat in Daniel's backyard and covered the whole street, but there was no sign of their friend. They were just on their way home for lunch when they heard the commotion.

"You little monster!" It was Jamie, shouting.

"Stay back! Or mine will poke yours to the death!"

In less than a heartbeat, Daniel and Talia were running down the path and into Talia's yard. They found Jamie, sprawled on the grass in front of his homemade pigeon trap, rubbing at his eye… and Megabat, behind the bars. His fur was ruffled and he was ferociously wielding his juice-box-straw lightsaber.

10

BIRDGIRL

"You almost stabbed me in the eye, you dumb bat!" Jamie shouted.

"Let that be a warning to yours!" Megabat bellowed from inside the pigeon trap.

"Stop!" Daniel yelled, putting himself between Jamie and Megabat. "Don't hurt my bat."

"*That's* your pet bat?" Jamie said.

"He's not a pet. He's called Megabat," Talia said. "And he's our friend."

"I'm telling Mom you've been playing with a talking bat!" Jamie said. "I bet she'll take it to the humane society *and* make you get a rabies shot."

"Don't you dare tell!" Talia said. "Or else."

"Or else what?" her brother taunted. "You'll sic your bat on me?"

Inside the cage Megabat was striking his most threatening pose. His tiny snout was twisted into the cutest little sneer.

Daniel bent down and reached his fingers through the bars. That was when he noticed three pigeons huddled at the back of the cage.

"Okay, look," Talia said. "Promise not to tell and I'll be your servant for a week." Jamie looked unimpressed. "Fine, a month."

"What does that include?" Jamie asked.

"The usual. Fetching your things, doing your bidding, picking up your dirty socks. But, in exchange, you don't say a word to Mom and the bat goes free."

"The pigeons too," Daniel added.

Jamie ran his tongue over his teeth while he considered the offer. "Fine."

Talia opened the latch and Megabat hopped into her hand.

Meanwhile, the three pigeons stepped out, bobbing their heads nervously. Jamie stomped and two of them flew off, but the third—with an all-white head and brown wings—strutted over and pecked at the strap of his sandal.

"Get lost!" Jamie kicked at it, but the pigeon didn't go.

"Why isn't it flying away?" Talia asked Jamie. "Did you hurt it?"

The pigeon didn't look hurt. It started preening its feathers.

"Birdgirl, yours is free now," Megabat said to the pigeon.

"Birdgirl?" Daniel said.

"Yes. This is being Birdgirl." Megabat sighed. "Ours met in yonder leafy tree," he explained. "Megabat offered Birdgirl a seed, which hers gobbled most hungrily and, sincely, Birdgirl has not left Megabat's side."

"Coo-woo." The pigeon tilted her head and looked at Megabat with obvious adoration.

"Servant!" Jamie barked. "Fetch me a ginger ale. And make it cold. Also, chips and salsa, but not the spicy kind."

"Yes, Master," Talia answered miserably.

Jamie raised his eyebrows and cupped one hand around his ear like maybe he'd misheard.

"I mean, yes *Grand Master Jamie of the Universe*. Come help me," she said to Daniel. "And put Megabat in your pocket. I don't trust my brother with him for a second."

In the kitchen, Patricia was at the table drinking coffee with a woman wearing purple dangly earrings.

"Oh, hi, Daniel." She set her cup down. "This is Catherine. She just stopped by to chat before she leaves on vacation."

Talia waved at her mom's friend, then she opened the fridge and grabbed a ginger ale for Jamie—plus a juice box for Megabat.

"I'm going to Borneo for a month to a drumming circle retreat," Catherine explained.

Daniel and Talia glanced at each other.

"I leave tomorrow." She jangled her earrings in excitement.

"Can you believe that?" Talia whispered, once she'd dragged Daniel into the family room. "This is our big chance to get Megabat home—and away from Jamie! All we need to do is slip him into Catherine's purse."

Daniel had visited his cousins in Vermont before, so he knew about airports. The security guards checked every bag by putting it through an X-ray machine. And even if Megabat *did* manage to slip through undetected, what if Catherine reached into her purse for a breath mint on the plane and pulled out a bat?

"Her purse is by the front door," Talia said. "It's now or never."

Daniel didn't feel good about the plan—but he knew they might not get another chance.

"What do you think, Megabat?" he asked. "Do you want to go back to the land of Papaya Premium now?"

"Undoubtedly," Megabat said solemnly. "Megabat will go in jingle-ears' purse. But mine will never forget yours." At that, Megabat's big, round eyes grew shiny.

There wasn't time for tears. Daniel started for the hallway. But before they'd taken two steps, they heard a dull thud, followed by a scream.

"What was that?" came Talia's mom's voice.

"I think a pigeon just flew into your glass door," Catherine answered.

Thud. Thud. Thud.

"I'm going to shoo it away before it knocks itself out," Catherine said. Then there was another scream.

If they'd been thinking clearly, Daniel and Talia might have seen this as the perfect opportunity to sneak

Megabat into the purse, but all the commotion was upsetting—especially to Megabat.

"Birdgirl is being in trouble!" Megabat said. He flapped toward the kitchen. By the time Daniel and Talia caught up, he was swooping around a pendant light. He narrowly avoided Catherine, who was waving a broom around, and landed on top of the kitchen cabinets where Birdgirl was huddled.

Megabat hopped onto the pigeon's back and held on tight. She was so upset by all the shouting and broom waving that she didn't know the way out, but Megabat pointed calmly with one

wingtip. Then Birdgirl, piggybacking Megabat, took off and sailed right through the open screen door.

The kitchen fell silent for a moment. "Did that really just happen?" Catherine asked Patricia. They both burst out laughing. "You always say your house feels like a zoo, but this is too much."

"Quick. Close the door," Patricia said. "Before they come back."

Talia closed it, then she looked at Daniel and sighed. He sighed back.

The purse plan hadn't been perfect, but it had been their best bet—and the pigeon had ruined everything. What were they supposed to do *now*?

11

TRAVELLING BAT

After lunch, Daniel found the bat
hanging upside down from his usual
place in the attic. But he wasn't alone.

"Coo woo. Coo wooooooo."

"You!" he shouted at Birdgirl. "Get
lost!" Birdgirl edged closer to Megabat.

"You ruined everything." Daniel
grabbed a comic book off his shelf and
waved it at her. The pigeon flew around

the room, bumping into a lamp and knocking a pile of books off the bedside table. Finally, she found her way out the window.

"Shoo!" Daniel said, shutting it. But Birdgirl stayed right outside, looking in.

Daniel flopped down on his bed and banged his head on the sloped attic wall. "I hate this room!" he yelled in frustration. "I hate this house! I hate this whole place! And I hate that stupid pigeon!" He felt so hopeless that he started to cry, and—*drip, drip, drip*—he wasn't the only one.

Daniel held out one hand and Megabat swooped down to nestle in his palm. There was something about the small weight of him there that made Daniel feel a little less alone—and somehow that helped a lot.

They stayed there for a while, neither of them feeling much like talking. Until—*thud, thud, thud*—Birdgirl began launching herself at the window.

Daniel had to admit that Talia's brother was right about one thing: pigeons *were* pretty dumb.

"Birdgirl is most distressed also," Megabat said with a little sniff.

"Well, she should be. She ruined our purse plan. She is *not* my favorite pigeon right now."

Daniel put Megabat back to roost on his beam then started picking up all the books Birdgirl had knocked over. There, at the top of the pile, was his *Children's Own Atlas*. Birdgirl's flapping had left it face-down on the floor, open to a page with two kinds of world maps. Daniel studied them. In the first map, Borneo was about as far away as you could get from North America. But in the second, which looked at the Earth from the other side, it was closer.

He measured both distances with his thumb. It took twelve thumbprints to go across the Atlantic to Borneo, but just seven to cross the Pacific Ocean.

Daniel knew that seven thumbs was still a long way… thousands and thousands of miles, probably… but it gave him an idea.

Megabat soon fell asleep, and Daniel went back next door. Talia's mother said she was upstairs playing with Jamie—but playing wasn't what Daniel would have called it.

From the top of the stairs, he could see Talia kneeling on the floor with a bucket of water and some sponges.

"Don't forget to wash between my toes," Jamie commanded.

"Hi," Daniel said, coming to stand in the doorway. "Can I talk to you for a minute? It's kind of important."

"Can't you see my servant's busy?" Jamie barked.

"I'm allowed to talk to people." Talia said.

"Fine." Jamie pulled his feet out of the bucket and walked toward the door, leaving wet footprints behind. "Just like I'm allowed to talk to people. Like, say, Mom… and tell her about your talking bat."

"Don't you dare!" Talia said, but it was obvious from his smirk that he *would* dare. "Just let me talk to Daniel for five minutes, okay? Then I'll organize your comic books *and* put your laundry away."

"And file my toenails," Daniel added.

"Fine," she said, then she motioned for Daniel to follow her into her room.

"I think I have a new plan for getting Megabat home," Daniel said once the door was closed. "He might be able to fly there himself—*if* we train him. He'll need to learn geography and survival skills. Plus practice his flying. It's a long journey."

"Seven thousand, five hundred and seventy miles," Talia said. Daniel looked at her in surprise. "I looked it up. I've been thinking the same thing," she explained. "But do you really think he can do it?"

"It might be our last hope."

"I think you're right," Talia said. She sat down on the bed. "I'll help train him as much as I can," she said. "But I'm going to be pretty busy."

"Talia!" Jamie shouted. "Time's up!"

"See? I'd better go. But I can come help on the days Jamie's at swimming lessons. And after dinner."

"Okay," Daniel said, even though he was feeling less certain about his plan by the second. Training a bat to fly across the world… Where was he supposed to start?

12

BAT SCHOOL

The next morning, Daniel and Megabat
went to the basement for the first
geography lesson.

Daniel started by drawing Megabat a
map of Borneo on his dad's whiteboard,
but the bat just scratched his head and
asked for apple juice.

They moved on to the cardinal
directions. "The letters you need to

know are N, E, S and W." Daniel drew them on the whiteboard. "They stand for north, east, south and west."

Megabat was busy licking one of his talons.

"So?" Daniel prompted. "What are the cardinal directions?"

"Yours said what?" Megabat blinked.

"Cardinal directions," Daniel repeated.

"Cardinal is being a bird!" Megabat answered triumphantly. "Theys is most red and chirpy."

Birdgirl, who was never far from Megabat (even though she wasn't allowed in the house), was sitting outside the closed basement window. She bobbed her head, as if agreeing.

"Not *that* kind of cardinal. Remember… north, south, east and west. Here's a good way to remember: Never Eat Shredded Wheat." It was a trick

Daniel's second grade teacher had taught the class. "See? The letters make the same sounds."

"Shredded wheat?" Megabat asked, puzzled. "Is most dust-gusting?"

"Well, kind of. It's mushy. But that's not the point. It's a way to remember the four letters."

"Megabat will be remembering," the bat promised vaguely, then he went back to cleaning his talons. "Shredded wheat," he muttered, between licks. "Most dust-gusting."

Daniel sighed.

"Buttermelon now?" Megabat asked, for the third time. Daniel had brought down a container filled with fruit to reward Megabat, but it only seemed to be distracting him.

"One piece," Daniel said. "Then we keep working."

While Megabat devoured his melon, Daniel worried about what to do next. Just then, the vent above him came on, letting out a blast of air conditioning.

Daniel shivered, then he stood up and walked toward some unpacked boxes. He found one marked "Coats & Gloves," opened it and lifted out his dad's old brown wool coat. The sleeves hung over his fingertips, but at least it was warm. He put up the hood.

"Okay, Megabat," he said. "Let's look at the map again."

Megabat glanced up from his piece of melon and gasped. "Jedi Master," he said, bowing low.

Daniel laughed. The big brown coat *did* kind of look like the cloak Obi-Wan wore when he trained Luke Skywalker. He was going to explain that it was just his dad's old winter jacket, but then he had an idea. He bowed back. "The Force is strong with you."

Megabat ruffled his wings with pride.

"Shall we begin your training now, young Jedi knight?" Daniel asked.

And so they did.

13

THE NORTH STAR

Daniel wore his dad's coat all week—
even in the blazing sun—and he and
Megabat kept training. The bat flew
laps of the block with Birdgirl at his side
and did wingtip push-ups to gain
strength.

He also worked with Talia whenever
she could come over, playing a game
called Can You Eat It?

It was Friday after dinner, and it was getting dark, but because it was the night before Megabat's big journey they were still hard at work.

"Cantaloupe?" Talia showed Megabat a flashcard.

"Eating it," Megabat answered, drooling.

"A used Band-Aid?"

"Not eating it." Megabat wrinkled his snout.

She showed him another flashcard. "Unidentified red berries?"

"Not eating it," answered Megabat. "Unless," he added, "it is smelling most delicious."

"No, don't eat it," Talia corrected.

"You could get sick."

"Oka-hay," Megabat agreed. "Also," he added gravely, "never be eating shredded wheat. Is most smushy."

Talia looked confused, but Daniel laughed out loud. "Okay," he told Megabat. "Go channel the Force now."

Megabat flew to the backyard shed. He hung upside down from the eaves and closed his eyes. Birdgirl perched on the roof above him. They looked peaceful in the moonlight.

"Tomorrow's the big day," Talia said. "Do you think he's ready?"

"I don't know," Daniel answered. "He still doesn't understand the cardinal directions."

"He *is* a bat. Maybe he can navigate by echolocation," Talia suggested.

"I thought of that," Daniel said, "but fruit bats don't use echolocation."

Daniel wasn't sure how they navigated. His books didn't say. Giving up, he lay back on the grass and closed his eyes.

"Aaaaaaaahhhhh!" came Megabat's voice suddenly. "Daniel! Talia! Looking!"

Daniel opened his eyes. "Oh!" he exclaimed. A shooting star had just streaked across the sky.

They sat silently together, watching for more.

"The Big Twinkly is much bright tonight," Megabat said.

"You mean the North Star?" Daniel said, pointing to the brightest light in the sky.

"Mm-hmm. Much twinkly," Megabat said… "perhaps mine bat brothers and sisters is watching it also."

That was when Daniel realized. "Megabat?" he said. "Which way is Papaya Premium?"

Megabat pointed absently behind him and to his left with one wingtip.

Of course! Fruit bats were nocturnal. It made perfect sense that Megabat could navigate using the stars.

Daniel grinned at Talia. She grinned back. And for the first time in a long time, he felt almost content. Megabat was going to make it home. Daniel was certain of it.

14

THE DEPARTURE

"Wake up!" Daniel said the next morning. "I have a surprise for you."

The bat opened one big eye. "Did yours say sumprise?"

Daniel held up a harness he'd made using some of his mom's fabric-covered hair elastics. "It's a holster for your lightsaber. So you can carry it while you fly."

Daniel stretched the elastic bands over Megabat's wings and attached the straw.

"Thanking yours," the bat said.

"You're welcome. Now come on," he added, before either one of them could get too sad. "We'd better go."

"There you are!" Talia said when they pushed open the gate to her yard.

"We're only a minute or two late." Daniel squinted at the sun. Even though bats were nocturnal, they'd decided Megabat should leave at first light. He'd fly by day and keep watch for predators, then get his bearings from the stars before finding safe places to sleep.

"Sorry. Jamie's waiting for me to run his bubble bath and he'll lose his patience if I take too long."

"Well, as soon as Megabat gets away, you can quit this whole servant thing, right?" Daniel said.

"Exactly." Talia smiled. "He can run his own dumb bath." Then she turned to Megabat. "Are you ready?"

"Undoubtedly," Megabat said.

"Cooo-wooo. Cooo-wooo." Birdgirl strutted around Talia's ankles, making the occasional fluttery jump toward the big bag of bread crusts she was holding.

Daniel and Talia knew the pigeon would try to follow Megabat, so they'd decided to distract her. She was going to be heartbroken when she realized Megabat had left, but she'd only slow him down on his journey. It was for the best.

"Well," Talia said sadly… "I guess this is goodbye." She took Megabat off Daniel's finger, scratched his ears and kissed him gently on the cheek.

"Goodbye, Talia," the bat answered. Then he flew back to Daniel and bowed. "Farewell, Master Daniel."

Daniel hesitated for a second, then stuck out his tongue and licked Megabat across the face. It was a little furry but, otherwise, not so bad. Daniel cleared his throat to keep from crying. "May the Force be with you," he said.

Talia scattered the bread on the grass, and as soon as Birdgirl started eating, Megabat flapped his wings once, twice, and took off into the cloudless sky.

But a moment later—*THUNK*—something landed at Daniel's feet.

"Did I catch him?" came a familiar voice. Jamie was leaning out the upstairs window. "I did!"

"Helping mine!" came the bat's panicked voice. Megabat was caught in a net Jamie had dropped. He was flapping frantically, getting more and more tangled.

"I heard what you said about running my own bubble bath." Jamie called. "Fat chance! The bat stays here. You'll be my servant for life."

"Quick," Talia said to Daniel. "Set Megabat free. I'll deal with Jamie." She ran into the house.

Meanwhile, Daniel went into Talia's garden shed. He found a small pair of yard clippers. "Keep still," Daniel told Megabat. The bat whimpered softly as Daniel made a first cut in the net. Then another. After one more snip, he pulled the netting from Megabat's left wing... but now he could see that it was even more tightly tangled around the right wing.

"Cooo-woooo? Coo woo woo woo." Birdgirl paced around Daniel in

nervous circles, making it hard to focus.

"Ohhhhh," Megabat moaned. "Hurting."

"Sorry," Daniel said. "It'll feel better once I get this off."

The back door of Talia and Jamie's house slid open. "Just come and see it yourself, Mom," he heard Jamie say. "It really *is* a talking bat."

"He's being stupid," Talia said. "There's no such thing." But a moment later, Patricia stepped onto the back deck.

"Daniel? What have you got there?" she asked.

Daniel didn't have to answer.

She took a step back. "It's another bat! Get away from it!"

Daniel made one last snip.

"Ahhhhh!" Megabat cried. The net fell away.

For a moment, Daniel thought everything would be okay... but then he saw the sheen of blood on the bat's wing and—worse—smelled its sharp metallic tang.

"Shoo." Patricia grabbed a broom and waved it around.

Megabat's and Daniel's eyes met. Daniel could tell his friend was scared, but the bat flapped his wings once, twice, three times and took off.

Birdgirl went after him.

And by the time Patricia reached the bottom of the steps with her broom, the bird and the bat were two silhouettes, heading south in the morning sky.

15

THE RETURN

Over the next two days, Daniel and Talia talked about Megabat constantly. In fact, Daniel's mind was so busy with thoughts of his little friend that he nearly forgot about the first day of school.

"Daniel!" his mom called up the attic stairs, three mornings after Megabat had left. "You don't want to be late."

His new school was on the corner near

his house, and by the time he'd laced up his running shoes, the street was filled with the familiar sounds of school bus engines and kids shouting—only, as familiar as it was, it seemed strange and scary too. Besides Talia and Jamie, Daniel didn't know anyone.

Talia wasn't in his class and the day dragged on. Daniel was relieved when the bell rang. He was hoping to hang out with Talia, but when he ran into her near the door, she was laughing with two other kids.

"Daniel, this is Nico and Ella," she said. "They're coming to play on my trampoline. You can come too if you want."

"Yeah," said the kid named Nico.

"We're playing popcorn."

"You can be the popcorn first," Ella added with a small smile.

Daniel didn't know that game… or if being the first popcorn was good or bad. Truthfully, he'd been hoping to talk more about Megabat. And, anyway, Talia's friends were probably only inviting him to be nice.

"Actually," he said, "I think I'm just going to go home today. See you later."

Talia frowned, but she didn't argue.

"Okay," she said. "See you later."

That night, to celebrate his first day of school, Daniel's mom made Japanese-

style spare ribs and his dad cooked them on the BBQ. They'd just finished setting the table on the patio when—

"Hey!" Daniel jumped. A little piece of gravel had hit him on the head.

Daniel's dad shielded his eyes and looked toward the sun. "Did that pigeon just drop rocks?" he asked.

More rocks fell. This time, a few landed in the salad bowl. Daniel wondered and hoped, then he squinted. Yes! The pigeon had an all-white head and brown wings. Birdgirl was back!

"So much for eating outside. Grab the food," his mom said. "Bring the last two plates, will you, Daniel?" Daniel nodded then watched his parents go inside.

"Birdgirl!" he whispered loudly. She landed at his feet.

"Coo-woo." She tilted her head from side to side. Then Daniel saw: attached to her back with Megabat's juice-box-straw holster was a black lump with limp, leathery wings.

For a moment, Daniel's heart seemed to stop, but then he saw that his friend was still breathing. He unstrapped the bat from the pigeon's back and cradled him carefully in his palm.

"Are you coming?" His mom leaned out the back door.

"Just a minute," he said. "I want to—uh—pick some flowers for the table."

He walked across the yard, opened the shed and set Megabat on top of a ceiling beam where he'd be safe. The bat shivered slightly, so Daniel pulled off one of his socks and tucked Megabat inside it like a sleeping bag. It was stinky, but it would have to do.

Birdgirl flew onto the beam and wrapped one wing over the bat.

"I'll be back soon, Megabat," Daniel whispered.

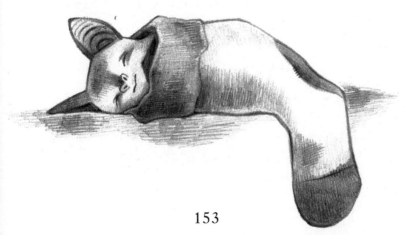

16

THE RECOVERY

When he was done dinner, Daniel asked if he could go play with Talia.

"It's Megabat," he whispered, when she opened the door. "He's in my shed."

He'd worried, at first, that Talia might not help him since he'd sulked off after school, but she didn't even hesitate.

"I'll meet you in five minutes," she answered—but she was there in two, carrying a first aid kit. She climbed onto a lawn chair. "I'm going to need a bowl of warm water and a clean sponge," she said. "A juice box too. He needs liquids."

By the time Daniel got back with the supplies, Talia had already done an examination.

"It's not good," she reported. "See? He lost his right wingtip."

Daniel felt sick. He'd suspected that he'd injured the bat badly when he cut the net, but now he knew for sure.

"He wouldn't have made it back without Birdgirl." Talia dipped the sponge into the bowl of water and squeezed it over the hurt wingtip. "He might never fly again," she added sadly.

"We'll check on him tomorrow, okay?"
Talia hopped off the lawn chair. "He'll
probably be awake by then."

Except he wasn't. That day and the
next, Megabat didn't open his eyes.

Talia came often to check on him,
and Daniel spent as much time as he
could with his friend, but Birdgirl was

Megabat's best nurse. The only time she left his side was to gather twigs to build a strong, warm nest around him.

It wasn't until five days after Megabat's return that he finally awoke.

Daniel had found a juicy purple plum in the fruit bowl. He was carrying it across the yard, hoping the smell might wake his friend, when he heard Megabat's voice.

"Oh. Now yours is being silly," the bat was saying.

Daniel's heart leapt with joy—Megabat was better! But would his friend even want to see him after what he'd done?

There was a rustling noise and the snapping of a twig. "Yours is not needing to be building this nest all alone. Giving that here, peeze." There was a long pause—then some soft, sad cooing.

"Fine, fine. Mine is sorry. Yes, yes, Birdgirl is only trying to be helping."

Daniel peered through the doorway just in time to see Megabat wrap his good wing over Birdgirl's back.

The bat nuzzled his snout against the pigeon's cheek. "Yours is a pretty bird. Megabat is not meaning to lose patience." Birdgirl ruffled her feathers, then closed her eyes.

Daniel took a step back. He didn't want to interrupt this private seeming moment, but his hand moved the shed door, making it squeak.

Megabat looked up. "A Daniel is here!" he said. "Birdgirl, looking!"

"Um. Hi." Daniel stepped into the dimness of the shed. "You're awake. How's your wing?"

Megabat lifted his bandaged wing, wincing. "Most hurty."

Daniel put the plum down on the

rafter beside Megabat. It seemed like such a small offering.

"I'm really sorry I cut you," Daniel said. "It's all my fault you can't go home."

Birdgirl edged closer and cooed something in Megabat's ear. He lifted his hurt wing a little, then let it drop. "Megabat cannot be flying anymore?" he asked.

Daniel shook his head.

All of a sudden, a tear slid down Megabat's cheek. Then another and another. Before long, there was a puddle on the dirt floor.

"Please don't drip, Megabat," Daniel pleaded.

Then Daniel started crying too. *Drip*

drip drip drip. Now both their tears were making a big, muddy mess.

"I'm so sorry," Daniel said. "I didn't mean to. I love you so much. I ruined everything and now you're stuck here forever."

At that, Megabat gave a little gasp. His long tongue darted out and licked up one of Daniel's tears before it could hit the ground. "Hey!" Daniel said.

"None more dripping," said the bat sternly. His tongue darted out again, licking up another of Daniel's tears.

"Stop that!" Daniel laughed.

"A Daniel is loving Megabat?" the bat asked sheepishly.

Daniel shifted uncomfortably and

cleared his throat. "Of course. I mean, you're my best friend in this town. I really missed you when you were gone."

"But yours did helping mine go all the same?"

Daniel nodded.

"But you probably would have been better off without me," he said. "I mean, look what happened."

"Look what happened," the bat repeated. He paused, deep in thought. "Megabat was lost and all alone, but Master Daniel did take him under his wing. He used-ed all his powers to help Megabat. But oh no! The evil Jamie was attacking! All hope was lost… but wait!" Megabat struck a fighting stance.

"A Daniel and Megabat did channel the Force!" He grabbed his lightsaber straw with his talon and slashed at the air. "A Daniel cutted free Megabat's wing and in a daring upwards exscape mine did evade the evil Jamie's net!"

Daniel couldn't help smiling. When Megabat told it like that, it *did* sound kind of heroic.

The bat got quiet for a second. He lifted his bad wing. "Megabat is not flying anymore," he said again, as if letting it sink in. "Is oka-hay."

For a while the only noise in the shed was Birdgirl, shredding sticks in the corner.

"Asking yours something?" Megabat said, in a hushed voice.

"Sure," Daniel answered. "Anything."

Megabat glanced at Birdgirl to make sure she wasn't listening.

"Does yours think Birdgirl is loving Megabat too?"

Bats don't blush, but the way Megabat's shoulders were hunched up in embarrassment made it clear he would have been blushing if he could.

"I don't know *anything* about pigeons—or girls," Daniel said. "But even I can tell she's crazy about you."

"And a Daniel is *muchly* loving Megabat," he said, like he needed to confirm it.

"Yeah, yeah," Daniel said. "Don't let it go to your head."

The bat straightened out his back. "Then Megabat is not needing the land of Papaya Premium," he said, looking around the shed. "Megabat is home."

"You mean, you *want* to stay?" Daniel asked. "With me? And Birdgirl?"

"And Talia," he added. "It's is oka-hay?"

Daniel didn't mean to, but suddenly he found himself dripping again, just a little. "Of course," he said. "Actually, it's kind of better than oka-hay."

17

A NEST FOR TWO

Late summer turned to fall. Megabat's
wingtip healed, leaving a silvery scar.
One day, he found he could glide from
the rafter to the shed floor. He worked
up to crossing the yard, then circled the
block with Birdgirl at his side. He landed
with shaking wings and bowed. Talia and
Daniel applauded.

When the weather got colder, Daniel

asked Megabat if he'd like to come back to live in the attic—but Megabat hunched his wings in embarrassment.

"Birdgirl," he said, "is keeping Megabat warm at night."

Daniel didn't ask any more questions about *that*.

Daniel was sure Megabat still missed his bat brothers and sisters— just like Daniel still missed his friends in Toronto—but they didn't talk about it as often, and neither of them dripped much. Daniel even made a few new friends at school.

Really—life was good, except for one minor detail.

It was a few weeks before Christmas

and the friends were hanging colored lights in the shed when the door burst open.

"I wondered what you guys were doing back here!" There stood Jamie wearing a fur-lined hat and his usual sneer. "It's the bat, isn't it? He's back! Talia, if you don't agree to be my servant for life, I'm telling Mom!"

"You leave Megabat and Talia alone!" Daniel put his hands on his hips.

"Or else what?" Jamie challenged.

Suddenly, Daniel had an idea. With a subtle flick of his wrist, he motioned to Birdgirl. She landed on his shoulder. He whispered in her ear and she took off out the door into the wintry air.

"Jamie," Talia said, "just go home, okay?"

"Fine..." he said. "I *will*. But only to get Dad's cell phone so I can record the talking bat and show Mom."

As soon as he left, Talia sat down in the wheelbarrow. "Great. What are we going to do now?"

"Just wait for it," Daniel said.

"Wait for what?" Talia asked.

A minute later they heard a commotion outside the shed. It sounded like a helicopter landing. Daniel threw open the door to reveal Jamie, running back toward them with a cell phone, already recording. In fact, he was so busy looking at the screen that he didn't notice the huge flock of pigeons at first.

"Shoo," Jamie said, waving his arms as the first one crossed his path. "Get lost," he said when a second one swooped past his ear.

"Coo-woo!" Birdgirl called.

That was when the pooping began. And not just regular pooping. *Massive* pooping. Every pigeon in the air—and there were almost a hundred—let loose at the same time.

"No!" Jamie tried to cover his head. "Gross! Make them stop!"

"They'll stop if you leave Megabat alone," Daniel shouted. "For good. And no more making Talia be your servant, or else they'll get you… every time you go outside."

"Okay, okay. Fine," Jamie said.

"Coo-woo!" Birdgirl ordered. The pigeons dispersed in the air like confetti.

"Clever, clever bird," Talia said, as

Birdgirl came back to roost in the shed.

"Yes," Daniel agreed, "the cleverest."

Megabat flew up to perch beside her. He bowed down low. "Birdgirl." He looked up at her adoringly. "Mine hero, mine love. Will yours marry Megabat?"

"Coo-woo!" She flapped her wings. It was a definite yes.

Then the four friends watched as Jamie picked up his pigeon-poop covered hat and ran from the yard.

"Coo-woo," Birdgirl said, contentedly.

"Yes," agreed Megabat. "A muchly happy ending."

A Little Bit about Bats

Megabat is based on a real kind of fruit bat (or megabat) called the lesser short-nosed fruit bat. These bats are tiny, weighing between 21 and 32 grams—which is about as heavy as an AA battery, or a mouse—and live in South and Southeast Asia and Indonesia (Borneo), usually in rainforests, near gardens, near vegetation or on beaches.

Of course, even though Megabat is based on a real kind of bat, he's also made up. I don't need to tell you that actual bats can't talk... not even in the funny way that Megabat talks! But it might be worth mentioning that bats don't make good pets, either.

Bats are amazing creatures and an important part of our ecosystem. North American bats eat insects, and they're rarely dangerous to humans. So if you see a bat in the wild it's okay to observe it from a distance, but don't try to touch it or trap it!

A Mega List of Thanking Yourses

I started writing Megabat for my kids, Grace and Elliot, just after we moved to a new city. We were all feeling a little lost and lonely in a place that was brand new to us—plus, what was with that weirdo leak in the roof?!

Thankfully, we eventually figured it out (it wasn't bat tears—just a bad roofing job), and because of the warm welcome my husband, kids and I received from our neighbors, it wasn't long before our new city felt exactly like home. That's why this book is dedicated to the people of our street (both past and present): Christine, Steve, Alex, Olivia, Cheryl, Jude, Emery, Selah, Anne, Cara, R.J., Liam, Mason, Nina, Jay, Audrey, Henrick, Brian, Cathy, Denise, Mike, Erin, Erich, Sandra, Jeff and Austin.

Of course, once it was written, Megabat also needed a home. That's where my amazing literary agent, Amy Tompkins, came in and introduced Megabat to the wise, witty and wonderful Samantha Swenson at Tundra Books. Not only did she take this batty little book under her wing, but she saw it through production with help from an A+ team including Andrew Roberts, Christie Hanson, Liz Kribs and Sylvia Chan. I'm most grateful to them, as well as to Kass Reich, whose utterly adorable illustrations melt my heart a little every time I turn a page.

Finally, I'd like to give a big high five to the Ontario Arts Council for their support of Megabat, as well as for their ongoing support of the arts in Ontario.

ANNA HUMPHREY has worked in marketing for a poetry organization, in communications for the Girl Guides of Canada, as an editor for a webzine, as an intern at a decorating magazine and for the government. None of those was quite right, so she started her own freelance writing and editing business on top of writing for kids and teens. She lives in a big, old brick house in Kitchener, Ontario, with her husband and two kids and no bats. Yet.

KASS REICH was born in Montreal, Quebec. She works as an artist and educator and has spent the majority of the last decade traveling and living abroad. She now finds herself back in Canada, but this time in Toronto. Kass loves illustrating books for all ages, like *Carson Crosses Canada* and *Hamsters Holding Hands*. This is her first book about a bat.

Stay tuned for the next MEGA adventure . . .

MEGA
BAT

AND **THE FANCY CAT**